This book belongs to

Marcus Burt

Add. Saskkachewan Drive

Edmonton A.B.

Phone 4385362

This is a Bright Sparks Book.
First published 2000
Bright Sparks
Queen Street House,
4, Queen Street,
Bath, BA1 1HE, UK.
Copyright © Parragon 2000

Produced for Parragon Books by
Oyster Books Ltd, Unit 4, Kirklea Farm,
Badgworth, Somerset, BS26 2QH, UK

Illustrated by Andrew Geeson
Written by Marilyn Tolhurst

Printed in Italy

ISBN 1 84250 060 0

BIRTHDAY BEAR

Illustrated by Andrew Geeson

Bright ☆ Sparks

Rosie woke up, jumped out of bed and ran into Danny's room, "Guess what day it is!"

"It's Saturday," muttered Danny, grumpily. "And it's raining too."

"I know it's Saturday, silly," exclaimed an excited Rosie. "But it's my birthday!"

Rosie spotted Jack the postman coming up the path. She ran downstairs to meet him.

"There's nothing for you," he teased.

But Jack's bag was bulging!

"You can open your cards when Daddy comes in,"
laughed Mum. "But the birthday girl needs her breakfast first."

Rosie could hardly wait.

After breakfast, they all watched while Rosie opened a great pile of cards and presents.

"I've got a card from Conker," said Rosie and gave him a big kiss. "It's got his paw mark on!"

They spent the morning getting the house ready for Rosie's birthday party. They blew up balloons and hung up streamers until everything looked perfect.

"That looks lovely," announced Mum, finally. "I can see Joe down by the pond. Why don't you go and feed the ducks while I finish everything else?"

Danny and Rosie ran through the orchard and waved to Joe the farm worker. It had stopped raining but it was still very wet and muddy.

"Happy birthday, Rosie," called Joe.

When they reached the pond, Rosie noticed something floating at the edge of the water all tangled up in the weeds.

"What's that muddy blob over there?" she asked.

"I'll go in and see," said Danny, splashing into the pond and wading out towards the curious object. Dan took three steps, then stopped.

"Go on," called Rosie. "What's the matter?"

Danny began to giggle.

"I can't move," he said. "My boots are stuck in the mud!"

Rosie started to laugh too. Danny wriggled, pulled, twisted and turned, trying to free his boots from the mud.

Suddenly, Danny's foot slipped out of his boot and he sat in the water with a huge splash.

Joe came across to see what all the laughter was about and held out his hand to Danny.

"What's that muddy mess you're holding?" he chuckled.

"I don't know," replied a very wet and muddy Danny, pulling weeds out of his hair. "Here–you can have it, Rosie."

"It's a bear!" cried Rosie, cuddling the soggy bundle. "A poor muddy old bear."

"I wonder how he got there?" asked Danny.

Dripping wet and covered with mud, Danny and Rosie walked back to the house.

"What have you been up to?" laughed Mum. "And who is this little fellow?"

Mum took the bear from Rosie.

"Oh dear! I think all three of you need a bath before the party starts."

In no time at all, Rosie, Danny and the little
bear were ready for the party.

"Wow! Come and
see the cake, Rosie,"
said Danny. "It
looks brilliant!"

Rosie tied
a big yellow bov
around the
bear's neck and
sat him on the
window sill
to watch the party.

At bedtime, Rosie sighed, "That was the best birthday party ever. I love being five."

"Do you know what my best present was, Mummy?" she added.

"What was that?" asked Mum.

"It was that poor old muddy bear. I wish I could keep him."

"Well, we'll have to wait and see" said Mum. "He might belong to someone."

The next day, Rosie made a "Lost Bear" poster and Jack put it in the post office window. Nobody came to collect the bear, so Rosie adopted him.

Rosie made up lots of stories about how the bear got into the pond. But they never did find out.

"It doesn't matter where you came from," she told him. "You can live with us now. Billy Rabbit can be your best friend."

"What will you call him?" asked Danny.

"Birthday Bear, of course!"